TAYLOR-MADE TALES

THE DOG'S SECRET

TAYLOR-MADE TALES

THE DOG'S SECRET

by

ELLEN MILES

AN
APPLE
PAPERBACK

SCHOLASTIC INC.

New York Toronto London Auckland Sydney
Mexico City New Delhi Hong Kong Buenos Aires

No part of this publication may be reproduced, stored in a retrieval system, or transmitted in any form or by any means, electronic, mechanical, photocopying, recording, or otherwise, without written permission of the publisher. For information regarding permission, write to Scholastic Inc., Attention: Permissions Department, 557 Broadway, New York, NY 10012.

ISBN 0-439-59708-0

Title page art by Jonathan Bean
Book design by Tim Hall

12 11 10 9 8 7 6 5 4 3 2   6 7 8 9 10 11/0

Printed in the U.S.A.   40

First printing, January 2006

For Jean, with gratitude and affection.

Kathryn, Not Cricket

Cricket Dezago?"

Cricket didn't answer. She didn't even hear her name. She was gazing at the notebook on the new teacher's desk. It was a big red notebook with the words "Taylor-Made Tales" in golden cursive letters across the front. What was in that notebook? Cricket was dying to know.

Oliver poked a finger into her side. "Cricket," he whispered, pushing his glasses up. "He's calling on you."

"Cricket?"

The new teacher stood near the blackboard. His bushy gray eyebrows moved up and down as he said her name.

Cricket couldn't help staring at those eyebrows. Too bad staring was rude.

She guessed that somebody with a name like

Cricket would probably stare anyway. Somebody named Kathryn, on the other hand, wouldn't think of it.

"Kathryn," she said, rubbing the place Oliver had poked. "My name is Kathryn."

"Oh." The eyebrows danced around as the man frowned. "I was sure Ms. Nelson told me everyone calls you Cricket." He made a note on the attendance sheet. "Okay, Kathryn it is." He ran a long, skinny finger down the list. "Leo Murray?"

Cricket looked over at Leo. He was staring down at his desk. She poked him, just like Oliver had poked her.

Leo jumped. "Here," he said.

Mr. Taylor — that was the name he'd written in big block letters on the blackboard — went on taking attendance. He peered at each of Cricket's classmates in turn. Something about that look reminded Cricket of the way her grandfather's basset hound stared at her at mealtimes. Maybe it was the teacher's long, droopy mustache or his serious, big brown eyes. But Mr. Taylor wasn't built like a basset hound. Instead of being roundish and low to the ground, Mr. Taylor was long and tall and skinny. His arms and legs were long and skinny, his fingers were long and skinny, and even his nose was kind of long and skinny. He looked as different from short, plump Ms. Nelson as any human being could possibly look.

Now Ms. Nelson was gone. Ms. Nelson, with her calm voice and her kind smile and her big, warm hugs when you were feeling upset about something.

Not that Ms. Nelson had smiled at Cricket very often. She was more likely to frown and say, "Hush, Cricket." Or she would hold up one-two-three warning fingers as she waited for Cricket to settle down.

"Cricket is a lively girl, bordering on rambunctious," began one of her notes to Cricket's mom. Cricket had seen it, kind of by mistake. She didn't know what "rambunctious" meant until she looked it up. It meant "boisterous, disorderly." Cricket had to look up *those* words, too. All the words meant pretty much the same thing: She was too noisy, too active, too *Cricket*.

That was probably why Ms. Nelson had left. Too much Cricket.

No, Cricket knew that wasn't true. Ms. Nelson had left because she was going to have a baby just about any minute. And soon after that, she and Mr. Nelson were moving to Tucson, Arizona, which was a gazillion miles from their school in Bayside, Massachusetts. So it wasn't Cricket's fault.

Cricket wanted the next teacher to like her, really *like* her. She decided that her rambunctious days were over. She decided she would become the kind of student that a teacher would love, and she would do it one step at a time. Step One was to Be Mature, so she would have to give up her baby nickname. She'd been called Cricket since the day her mom had met her at an orphanage in China. She had been just nine weeks old, and her mom said she had squeaked like a cricket. But now that she was nine *years* old, it was time to use her real name, Kathryn. Kathryn was a polite, quiet kind of a girl. Kathryn was not disorderly or boisterous. Kathryn was certainly not rambunctious.

Kathryn was the kind of girl a teacher would love. And for once, Cricket wanted to be the one the teacher liked best. She wanted to be the one who got picked to help pass out things or bring a note to the principal's office. She wanted to make the teacher smile.

"Kathryn?"

Oliver poked Cricket again. "He's calling you."

Cricket jumped. She wasn't used to her new name. "Oh! Yes?" she asked.

"Do you have anything to share this morning?" Mr. Taylor asked. He peered at Cricket through his eyebrows, like an owl peering through the branches of a tree.

Cricket wondered what Kathryn would say at sharing time.

"Um, I saw a rabbit on my way to school this morning," Cricket answered. "A brown rabbit." It was about the safest, most boring thing she could think of to say.

Oliver stared at her. Cricket knew why. He was probably expecting her to tell about what she and her mom had for dinner last night, like fried tarantulas or boiled yak. Or maybe he was expecting her to show off her latest bruise or cut and tell how she got it. That was the kind of thing she usually did at sharing time. But Step Two in her plan was to Blend In, instead of sticking out. So no more boiled yak stories. It was too bad. Cricket liked to tell stories.

Mr. Taylor just nodded. He almost looked disappointed. He definitely looked bored. For a second, Cricket even thought he was going to yawn. "Okay," he said. He looked over at Leo. "Leo?"

Leo looked down at his desk. "Somebody called last night," he mumbled. "They said they saw a spotted dog near the playground. But it wasn't Tracker. It was too little."

"Is your dog missing?" Mr. Taylor asked.

Still looking down, Leo nodded. Cricket could tell he was trying not to cry. No wonder he looked so sad! Leo loved his dog. Cricket felt awful for him. Leo usually told his joke of the day during sharing time. Leo always found something to laugh about. But not today. "Tracker's been gone since Friday," he said in a whisper. "We put up signs and everything, but . . ."

Since Friday! Today was Monday. Cricket counted on her fingers. That was three whole days.

Mr. Taylor walked over to put a hand on Leo's shoulder. "I hope Tracker comes home soon," he said. Then he looked around at the rest of the class. "Has anyone else lost something important lately?" he asked.

"I did!" yelled Jason Tourville, without raising his hand.

But his twin sister, Jennifer, seemed a little suspicious. "Why?" she asked Mr. Taylor.

The other kids seemed to be wondering, too. Nobody really knew what to make of the new teacher. But whether or not she liked him, Cricket wanted the new teacher to like her.

Even though she couldn't think of anything she'd lost, Cricket raised her hand without yelling out. She thought that someone named Kathryn would always raise her hand. That was Step Three. Teachers love it when you Raise Your Hand. At the end of the row, Molly Hamilton did the same. But Mr. Taylor didn't call on either of them. Instead, he strode back to the front of the room. "I'll tell you what," he said. "How about if you each draw a picture of something you've lost?"

Almost before he'd finished, everybody jumped up and ran for the markers in the coffee cans on the arts-and-crafts shelf. The only person who didn't bolt for the markers was Cricket. She thought that a girl named Kathryn would wait until the teacher *said* they could get markers. (Step Four: Always Wait for Instructions.)

She waited for as long as she could stand it, but Mr. Taylor didn't say a thing about the markers. He was already sitting at his desk, leafing through the big red notebook. When he smiled down at one of the pages, Cricket started to wonder if it was possible to die of curiosity. She *really* wanted to know what was in that book. What in the world was a Taylor-Made Tale?

Then Leo came back with a handful of the best markers, the ones that smelled like tropical fruits. Cricket decided she'd waited long enough. She jumped up and grabbed the last lonely markers left in the can: a brown one, a boring navy blue one, and a gray one that she already knew was dried out.

Leo looked at the markers when she put them on her desk. He moved his markers over to the side of his desk so Cricket could reach them.

"Thanks," she whispered.

Leo just nodded. He was already hard at work on his drawing of Tracker, the little spotted dog who always wagged her whole body, not just her tail.

Cricket didn't know what to draw. Tapping a marker against her desk, she glanced around, hoping for an idea. It was amazing how different the classroom looked already. Ms. Nelson's last day had been Friday. Mr. Taylor must have been here all weekend, moving things around. There was a fish aquarium where the globe used to be. The globe was over by the computer area now, and the computer area was changed around. Now three people could work at the desk, not just one at a time. The giant model of Saturn that she and

Oliver had made was hanging over by their cubbies now, instead of near the blackboard. And the reading area — Mr. Taylor had changed that most of all.

The new reading corner looked so cozy that Cricket wished she could sneak over there right then. She wanted to pull a book from the shelf and settle in for a good read. Or maybe instead of a book from the shelf, she would take that notebook from Mr. Taylor's desk.

Then she looked down at her own desk and remembered: She was supposed to be drawing a picture. A picture of something she'd lost.

She glanced over to see what Oliver was drawing. It was a picture of a big boat sailing over blue water.

"What's that?" she whispered.

Oliver gave her a look over his glasses. "What do you think? It's a boat."

"You lost a boat? I didn't even know your family *had* a boat."

Oliver giggled. "We don't," he said. "It's a toy

boat. I used to play with it in the bathtub when I was little. I wanted to give it to Sophie, but I can't find it. Neither can my mom or dad."

Sophie was Oliver's baby sister. She was really cute, but wow, she sure could yell. She was *loud*. After spending an afternoon around Sophie, Cricket was usually glad she was an only child.

Cricket still didn't know what to draw, so she checked out Molly's desk. What had Molly lost? As far as Cricket could tell from her drawing, Molly had lost a lady in a blue dress.

"Who is that?" she whispered across the aisle.

Molly's face was kind of sad. "Ms. Nelson," she said.

"Oh," said Cricket. She should have known. Molly had *loved* Ms. Nelson, and Ms. Nelson had just adored Molly. Molly was the kind of student that teachers liked best: quiet, smart, polite. Personally, Cricket thought Molly was a little *too* quiet. She was like a nervous little mouse watching for a cat. Molly did not talk in class — especially not now, with a new teacher whom she was probably a little afraid of. She didn't laugh a lot, and she stayed away from loud boys like Jason.

Cricket turned around to see what Jason was drawing. Of course. It was a playing card, the ace of hearts. Cricket thought it was probably from Jason's favorite deck, the one with Garfield pictures on the back. Jason and his friends were crazy about cards. They played every chance they got: at snacktime, after lunch, and probably all day after school and on weekends. The big game was war, but they also played slapjack and rummy and crazy eights. Cricket played sometimes, and so did Jason's sister, Jennifer. But Jason played more than anyone.

Jennifer was drawing a picture of something heart-shaped. Cricket gasped and Jennifer looked up. "You lost your locket?" Cricket whispered. Everybody knew Jennifer loved her gold locket more than anything. It opened up, and there were places for two pictures inside. Jennifer had put her and Jason's baby pictures in there. Cricket didn't think that was so smart because they had been really, really ugly babies even though they were both normal-looking now.

Jennifer nodded. "It's probably just in my room somewhere," she whispered back.

Then Cricket saw Mr. Taylor looking at her. Oops. He'd only known her for about half an hour, and she was already ruining her perfect Kathryn reputation. She turned back, looked at her desk, and tried to think of something she'd lost.

"Two more minutes," said Mr. Taylor.

Cricket panicked. Then she remembered that she'd lost an old tennis ball the day before. She'd been playing fetch with her neighbor's dog. Quickly, Cricket drew a circle with the dried-up gray marker. She grabbed one of Leo's markers, a green one, and scribbled in some grass underneath the circle. There. That would have to do.

She shoved the picture aside and went back to staring at Mr. Taylor's red notebook. What was inside that book? It was so hard being Kathryn! Cricket would have just asked about the notebook right away. But Kathryn knew about Step Five: Wait Your Turn.

Mr. Taylor was walking around the room, looking at all the pictures and making little noises of "hmm" and "nice." When the teacher asked, Cricket had to explain that her circle was a tennis ball. She was embarrassed. It was such a dumb picture. It wasn't complicated like the boat Oliver had drawn or as important as Leo's picture of Tracker.

Then Jason spoke up. "Mr. Taylor," he asked, "what's that book on your desk?"

Cricket let out a long breath. Finally, somebody had asked!

"Stories," Mr. Taylor said simply. "They're stories I've told to other classes, at other schools."

"What about *our* class? Can you read one of them to us?" Jennifer called out.

Mr. Taylor shook his head. "I won't read one," he said. Everybody groaned — even Molly and Cricket-turned-Kathryn. Mr. Taylor didn't shush them. In fact, he acted as if he hadn't heard a thing. "I'll do better than that," he went on. "I'll tell you a story that isn't even in the book yet."

"Cool!" shouted Jason.

"When?" asked Jennifer.

"How about at your usual read-aloud time at the end of the day?" Mr. Taylor asked. "I know Ms. Nelson just finished reading you a book, so you're ready for something new, anyway."

"But that's not for *hours*!" Oliver complained.

Mr. Taylor smiled. "All the better," he said. "We'll have time to get some work done first."

"What's the story about?" Leo asked.

"Well," he said, "I'm looking around the room and getting some ideas." Mr. Taylor looked at the pictures on the kids' desks. "I think it will be about some of the very things you have drawn. It will be the story of a very special dog, a heart-shaped gold locket, the ace of hearts, a boat, and —"

Cricket held her breath, wishingwishingwishing he would pick her drawing. If he did, it would become part of his story.

"— a tennis ball."

The Story Begins

The day seemed to crawl by. Cricket thought two o'clock would never come. But finally, after they finished working on their Mexico projects, Mr. Taylor said it was time for the story.

"Let's get comfy," said Mr. Taylor, leading the way over to the reading corner. "Grab a pillow." He was carrying a purple mug that Cricket had seen him fill from a jug of water he kept by his desk.

The new, improved reading corner had a big pile of cushions. There were enough for everyone in the class to have one, and each was a different color and size. Cricket saw round striped pillows, square polka-dot ones, wild tie-dyed ones, and one that was really elegant: It was red satin with gold tassels at each corner. The pillows were piled on the floor near a big, comfy chair. The chair was covered in dark green corduroy so old that it was faded and soft. Next to the chair was a lamp with a painted shade. Mr. Taylor folded himself into the green chair, then snaked a long arm up to switch on the lamp.

Cricket stared. When the light went on, a whole scene popped into view! She saw a wide blue river with boats on it and thick forests lining its sides. There was a tiny cabin hidden away in the woods and a little black dog sitting in the yard of a big white house.

She was so busy looking at the amazing lamp that she forgot to run for the fancy red pillow, and Jennifer got to it first. But Cricket found a nice green one with purple polka dots, and she sat down next to Molly. She looked around the circle of faces.

Everybody looked a little nervous, a little unsure about Mr. Taylor. Jennifer sat with her arms folded and a prove-it-to-me look on her face. Jason played with a deck of cards. Leo had his chin in his hand — probably still thinking about Tracker, Cricket guessed. Oliver waited patiently for the story to start. And Molly sat as far away from Mr. Taylor as she could. Cricket, sitting next to her, wondered if her Kathryn plan was going to work with Mr. Taylor. So far, he didn't seem impressed.

If Mr. Taylor noticed that everyone was a little on edge, he didn't show it. He just smiled at everyone and started right in.

"So," said Mr. Taylor. "This is a story about Maisie and her dog, Jack, and how Jack learned —" He stopped himself. "Well, you'll find out."

He looked up at the ceiling.

He took a long, deep breath.

And then he began. His whole face lit up, and his voice got so quiet that Cricket really had to listen. She listened so hard she forgot she was in school. She forgot about wanting to be Kathryn. She forgot about everything except Mr. Taylor's story.

■ ■ ■

"There was once a girl named Maisie," he began....

At the time of this story, she was — oh, I guess she was just about your age. She was small and quiet and as quick in her movements as a little bird. She had shining brown hair, which she wore in two long, tidy braids. Maisie lived in a tiny town a lot like yours, only maybe even tinier. It was called Tinsdale, and it sat on the banks of a big, wide river.

■ ■ ■

"Like the river on the lamp?" Leo blurted out.

That was exactly what Cricket was wondering. She held her breath. Would Mr. Taylor get mad at Leo for interrupting? But Mr. Taylor just nodded and went on with the story.

Maisie and Jack

Maisie *put her book in her lap, marking her* place with a finger. Her dog, Jack, sat up and pricked his ears. The shouts and laughter from outside were louder now, which meant that the Ackermans were in the backyard. Maisie sighed and stroked Jack's silky ears as she gazed outside from her window-seat perch. Yes, there they all were, piling into their little yellow playhouse. She spotted Adam's dark hair, Andrew's tall frame, and Ali's long braids as the three oldest Ackerman kids ducked through the door. Arthur and Aaron were poking their heads out the windows and making faces. Annie laughed as she tried to copy them. Annie was the youngest.

Way up above them, Maisie sat in her snug attic hideaway. Maisie made faces, too. Without a mirror, she couldn't tell if she was getting it right, but it *felt* so silly that she burst into a giggle.

"Is that a funny book, darling?" Maisie's mother appeared in the doorway of Maisie's room. Then she heard the noise from outside. "Oh, honestly," she said, striding to the window and slamming it shut. "Don't they have *any* manners? Why do we have to live next door to the loudest, biggest family in Tinsdale?"

Maisie's mother and father could not stand the Ackerman children, nor their parents, for that matter. Mother thought the children were "loud, ill-bred, and really rather rough." Father said it was "just awful, the way that man has let his lawn go." They would not let Maisie play at the Ackermans' home, and they ignored Mr. and Mrs. Ackerman. Mother often said she never even could be sure how many Ackerman children there were.

"There are six, Mother," Maisie would say. Then she'd name them, from oldest to youngest. "Andrew, Alison, Adam, Aaron, Arthur, and Annie." She knew more than their names, too.

She knew all about them. Maisie knew that Ali liked to stay up reading; she knew that Annie hated having her hair washed; and she knew that Adam had recently lost his favorite baseball glove.

But the Ackerman children barely knew Maisie. She never rode on the school bus with them, because Mother drove her to school. She never played in their twilight games of hide-and-seek or kick the can. (According to Father, it was too dangerous for children to play alone outside at night.) And Maisie had never, ever been in their playhouse. She longed to go inside and look out through those blue-curtained windows.

The Ackerman children had invited her over at first. When Maisie and her parents had just moved into their much-too-big house, they had asked her to play. But after she said no a few times, they gave up. Maisie didn't blame them. What did they care? They had plenty of friends to play with right there at home.

At least Maisie had Jack. It was a miracle, really, that her parents had let her keep him. Aunt Betsy had surprised Maisie with Jack on her eighth birthday. Jack was just a puppy then. Maisie thought her parents might be a little afraid of wonderful, laughing Aunt Betsy and her big ideas. But when Aunt Betsy told them that Jack needed a good owner and said that Maisie would be perfect, Mother and Father had simply agreed.

Jack was almost two now, and full grown. What kind of dog was he? It was hard to say. He had the strong body and square head of a Labrador retriever, but his black coat was long and silky like a spaniel's. One ear stood up and one lay down, giving him a funny expression. He had a patch of white on his chest and one white paw. Jack, in other words, was a mutt.

But Jack was a mutt like no other. There was something about his eyes. Reddish-brown and bright, they didn't miss a thing as Jack watched the world around him. Maisie often wondered what her dog was thinking. He would sit and look out of the living-room window for hours, keeping track of the people who walked past the white picket fence in front of their house.

Jack never begged like other dogs. He just lay

there with his front paws crossed and his feathery tail trailing out across the floor behind him. He would be quiet but alert while Maisie and her parents ate their silent, polite dinners at the dining-room table.

Then Jack would follow Maisie up to her room, and Maisie would lay out cards on the the little red table near the window. Mother and Father thought she was reading — they loved to boast about their little bookworm — but she didn't always have her head in a book. In the evenings, Maisie liked to play cards. Aunt Betsy had taught her lots of different ways to play solitaire, and every night she played until she had won three times. Then she would shuffle the cards and set them neatly aside for the next night.

When she slipped under the covers, Jack would curl up on the cozy sheepskin bed on the floor near the foot of her bed. When Maisie turned out the light, they would join in a duet of sighs as they settled down to sleep.

Maisie wasn't exactly the happiest girl in the

world but, thanks to Jack, she wasn't the saddest, either.

■ ■ ■

Mr. Taylor stopped talking and cleared his throat. Cricket felt as if he'd broken some kind of spell. She was already so involved in the story that she'd forgotten that it *was* a story. She knew just how Maisie felt sometimes. Being an only child could get lonely, even if you had a nice mom like Cricket's. Poor Maisie had a couple of real stinkers for parents.

Nobody said a word. Nobody moved a muscle. Cricket could tell that everyone felt the same way she did: They just wanted to hear more about Maisie and Jack.

Mr. Taylor took a sip of water from his mug. Then he went back to the story.

Annie's Idea

One bright, sunny day in late June, Maisie and Jack were playing fetch in her backyard. Jack loved to dash across the lawn for his favorite chewed-up tennis ball, which was so old it was more gray than yellow. He also loved making Maisie chase after him to get back the ball.

■ ■ ■

Cricket glanced up quickly when Mr. Taylor mentioned the words "tennis ball." He was looking straight at her! She felt her face getting warm. Was that really the tennis ball she drew? She was dying to ask, but being Kathryn meant that she didn't dare interrupt. Mr. Taylor winked and gave her a tiny nod. Then he went on with the story.

■ ■ ■

Maisie was laughing out loud, trying to convince her dog that the whole point of the game of fetch was to return the ball to the person who'd thrown it. Instead, Jack was running around in circles. He waved his tail proudly as he showed off his prize.

"He acts like that old ball is something special," said someone behind Maisie.

Maisie spun around to see Arthur and Annie Ackerman peeking through the rosebushes that separated their two yards. Arthur was smiling and shaking his head as he watched Jack run.

"Can I throw it to him?" Annie begged.

Maisie gave a quick glance toward her house. She knew her mother was out at a committee meeting, and Father was putting in some extra time at the office. It was a little risky, since Mother might come home any minute, but all of a sudden, Maisie didn't care.

"Sure," she said, "if we can get it out of his mouth!"

Arthur and Annie climbed through a gap in the row of rosebushes. Jack came a little closer. He smiled a doggy smile at the newcomers, without letting go of the ball.

"That is the rattiest ol' ball I ever saw!" said Arthur. "Ugh!"

But Annie didn't seem to mind. She put out a hand. "Come on, Jack," she said. "Give it here."

Jack's ears perked up.

"How did you know his name?" Maisie asked.

"We hear you calling him," Arthur explained, watching as Jack moved closer and closer to Annie.

"*Good* boy," Annie said as Jack dropped the ball at her feet. She squatted down, picked it up in both hands, and threw it as far as she could, which wasn't very far at all. Jack sprinted for it, grabbed it on the run, and trotted back. Without even being asked, he dropped it again at Annie's feet. He took two steps backward and sat down with an expectant look at the little girl.

"Gosh!" said Maisie. "How did you make him do that?"

"Annie's great with dogs," Arthur said. "Too bad we can't have one. Dad's allergic."

Annie gave Jack's ears a rub. He leaned against her, totally content. "Sometimes I pretend that Jack is partly mine," she confessed.

Maisie felt a pang. Annie wanted a dog as much as Maisie wanted friends. "Sometimes I pretend that I'm part of your family," she blurted out. Annie looked surprised. Maisie was surprised, too. She had not meant to say that.

Arthur gave her a look. Even though he was at least a year younger than she was, Maisie could tell he understood.

Annie seemed to understand, too. She slipped a small hand into Maisie's. "You know what you should do?" she asked. "You should teach Jack to talk. Then you wouldn't be so lonely."

Maisie stared into Annie's eyes for a second. It made her feel very odd that this little girl seemed to know her so well. Then she gave her head a little shake. She didn't want Annie to feel sorry for her.

"I'm not that lonely," she declared.

Just then, Maisie heard a car pull into the driveway in front of the house. Mother was home! She turned to tell Annie and Arthur that they'd better go, but they were already climbing through the bushes.

That night, Maisie finished her last game of

solitaire and shuffled the cards for the next time. It was very quiet in her room. Outside, a car door slammed as a neighbor arrived home. A mourning dove hooted in the twilight.

Maisie looked down at Jack. His intelligent eyes met hers.

"Hmm," said Maisie.

■ ■ ■

"She's going to do it!" Jason blurted out. "Teach him to talk!"

"Dogs can't talk," Jennifer said scornfully.

"Did you ever try to teach one?" Mr. Taylor asked, with a little smile.

Lessons

Maisie decided to start the very next morning. The only problem was, she didn't know how to teach a dog to talk. She didn't have any idea! She thought it over while she was trying to get to sleep that night, and she thought some more first thing when she woke up. By the time breakfast was over, she had come up with a plan.

Maisie knew that when people teach a baby or someone from another country a language, they usually go word by word. They point at something, tell the person the word for it, and repeat it until the person understands. Maisie thought maybe she could do the same thing with Jack.

Maisie figured it would be simplest to start with words that would be easy for Jack to say. First thing after breakfast, she took him outside. She pointed up at the gray slate roof of their house. "Roof," she said. "Roof."

Jack sat there calmly, his tail curled neatly beside him. He looked at Maisie. He followed her gaze up to the roof. Then he looked at Maisie again.

"Roof," Maisie said a few more times.

Jack seemed to be listening. He even seemed to understand that she wanted something from him.

Maisie was patient. "Roof," she said one more time, pointing up to it. "Say it, Jack."

"Rrr-ooff," Jack barked.

Maisie nearly fell over. "Oh, Jack!" she cried. She reached into her pocket for a piece of cheddar cheese. She'd cut it up that morning, slipping into the kitchen while Mother was busy in another room. At the puppy-training classes she and Father had gone to, the trainer had talked about using treats to reward good behavior.

Maisie tossed a little chunk of cheese to Jack. "Good dog!" she said as he snapped it up.

Later that morning, Maisie took Jack for a walk. They both enjoyed strolling through town. They liked to see the sights — and Jack liked to smell the smells. That day, Maisie took every opportunity to teach Jack words.

Maisie saw a big barge down by the river. It was tied up to the dock so it could unload. Maisie pointed to the docking place. "Wharf," she told Jack. "Wharf."

Jack stared, first at Maisie and then at the wharf.

"Come on, Jack," she said encouragingly. "Wharf!"

"Whoorf!" Jack growled.

Maisie felt like dancing. This wasn't so hard, after all! She gave Jack some more cheese.

"Whoorf!" he said again. "Whoorf!" His eyes were bright with excitement.

All the way home, Maisie pointed things out. "Hoof," she said as they passed a horse at a little riding stable on a side street. "Rough," she told Jack, stroking the bumpy bark of the biggest maple in the village square. She pointed to its snaky old roots. "Root."

With a little encouragement, Jack repeated each

word. And every time he did, Maisie gave him a small piece of cheese and lots of praise. "I always knew you were a smart dog," she told him as they walked back toward home. "I just didn't know *how* smart."

They rounded the corner near home and passed the Wilsons' house, which was next door on the other side from the Ackermans'. The Wilsons' oldest daughter was out in the garden, pulling weeds from a bed of pink and white petunias.

"Good morning, Maisie," she called.

Maisie waved happily. "Good morning, Ruth!"

"Rr-uth!" Jack echoed.

Ruth Wilson sat back on her heels and stared at the dog.

But Maisie just smiled and waved again. Then she took Jack inside, opened the fridge, and gave him the rest of the cheddar. She could hardly believe how quickly Jack was learning. Maisie was so proud and happy she thought she might burst. From now on, life was going to be different. She'd never be lonely again — or so she thought.

■ ■ ■

"Tracker loves cheddar cheese," Leo said softly. His voice was so quiet, he was almost talking to himself.

Mr. Taylor paused in the story and nodded. "Most dogs do. Jack was crazy about it."

Molly raised her hand. "My dog *hates* cheese," she said in her little, whispery voice after Mr. Taylor called on her. "He only likes dog food. And sometimes cat food."

Cricket stared at her. Molly never talked that much!

Jennifer made a face. "Well, I just don't believe you can really teach a dog to talk," she sniffed. "That's ridiculous."

Mr. Taylor nodded again and smiled. "We'll see about that," he said, reaching up to turn off the lamp as the final bell rang. "Tomorrow."

Everybody groaned. How could the day be over already? And how could they go home without knowing what would happen next?

Found

Cricket walked home slowly that day, thinking about Mr. Taylor. He wasn't like any teacher she'd ever had before, that was for sure. She had a funny feeling, as if her heart was pounding just a little faster than usual. Things were going to be different from now on in good old room 3B.

When she got home, Cricket found a note from her mom on the kitchen counter. "Working," it said. "Done by 5:30. Have some cookies and milk. Mrs. C. wants you to walk Buck. Love and a million, trillion kisses, Mom."

Cricket's mom was a photographer for the local newspaper. She spent most mornings roaming all over town, taking pictures of store openings and of cats stuck up in trees getting rescued by firefighters. She spent most afternoons in the tiny darkroom that was tucked away under the stairs. There, she developed the beautiful black-and-white pictures that she tried to sell at art . galleries.

Cricket had a few cookies, then headed next door to get Buck, the neighbor's bouncy cocker spaniel. Mrs. Czaplinski paid her five dollars a week to walk him after school. Usually Cricket took him around the block, and then they played fetch in her backyard for a few minutes. But the tennis ball they'd lost yesterday had been her last one.

"Sorry, Buck," Cricket said when they finished their walk around the block. "No fetch today. We don't have a ball." But Buck didn't seem to hear her. He pulled at the end of the leash and dragged her toward a pot of red geraniums. "No!" said Cricket, trying to hold him back. "No peeing on the flowers."

But Buck didn't lift his leg. Instead, he shoved his nose into the pot and came up with a tennis ball in his mouth. It was the one they'd lost the day before! Cricket laughed. "Okay," she said, reaching for the ball. "You win."

After a long game of fetch, Cricket took Buck home. Then she went back to her house and knocked on the door of the darkroom.

"Almost done," her mom called. "Meet me in the kitchen in ten minutes."

Soon Cricket was setting two places on the counter while her mom started dinner.

"So, Mr. Taylor seems nice," said Cricket's mom. She pulled some lettuce out of the fridge.

"He is," said Cricket. "Wait, how do *you* know?"

Her mother put down a tomato. "He called me this afternoon."

Cricket stared at her. "What? Why?" It felt strange to think that her mom had been talking to her new teacher while she was out playing with Buck.

"Just to introduce himself, I guess. And"— Cricket's mom looked serious — "he was a little worried about you. He said you seemed much more quiet than he had expected. He wanted to know if anything was wrong." She paused and looked into Cricket's eyes. "Is it?"

Cricket shook her head, feeling miserable.

"No," she mumbled. "Everything's fine." She couldn't believe it. First she had a teacher who didn't like her because she was too noisy, and now Mr. Taylor thought there was something wrong with her because she was quiet! She couldn't win.

Cricket's mom nodded, picked up the tomato, and started slicing it. "Funny thing," she added. "He called you Kathryn. For a second there, I almost couldn't figure out who he was talking about."

Cricket shrugged and put on a fake smile. It seemed to convince her mom.

Her mom smiled back. "Well, you seem like regular old Cricket to me," she said as she tossed the tomato slices into the salad. "Ready for supper?"

Talented Dog

All day on Tuesday, Cricket tried to smile and seem happy whenever Mr. Taylor looked her way. By two o'clock, when it was finally read-aloud time, her cheeks hurt from grinning so much. She was glad when Mr. Taylor sat down in his chair, switched on the lamp, and began the story. Finally, she could stop smiling and just listen. Mr. Taylor picked up the story where he'd left off the day before, with Maisie teaching Jack to talk.

■ ■ ■

"Do you think we could go out and play fetch now?" Jack asked politely.

After just two weeks of lessons, Jack was speaking in complete sentences. Sometimes Maisie thought she must be dreaming. But no, it was true.

Jack had learned to talk.

Not only that, but he'd turned out to be an

excellent friend. Jack was funny and kind, and he had the best manners of anyone she had ever met. He thanked her over and over for the nice life her family had given him ever since Aunt Betsy had rescued him from the animal shelter.

Now that Jack could talk, Maisie didn't spend nearly as much time gazing out her window. Instead, she and Jack chatted for hours up in her room. They always spoke softly, keeping their voices low so Mother and Father wouldn't hear.

Maisie often wished she could tell *someone* Jack's amazing secret. The Ackermans, for example. She knew that they would think it was the most amazing, wonderful thing in the world to have a talking dog. And after all, the whole thing had been Annie's idea. But Maisie knew it was probably better to keep it a secret. Once word got out about a talking dog, Maisie wouldn't have him all to herself. He would be famous! And if he was off appearing on TV and meeting his fans, Maisie might even end up back where she was before, lonely and sad.

So when Jack and Maisie took their walks through town, Jack was quiet. But he paid attention. And when he and Maisie were safely back home in her room, he would make her laugh and laugh by pretending to be the townspeople they'd met. His imitations were never mean. They were just — perfect.

"Why, hello, Maisie," he'd say in the very proper voice of Miss Nancy, Maisie's ballet teacher. "Are you looking forward to our dance recital?"

Or, "Well, well, well, if it isn't my favorite little girl and her faithful companion," Jack would yell in the foghorn voice of Mr. Rispoli, who owned the hardware store.

And his imitation of the postmaster, Tess Twillingham, was so exact that Maisie could hardly look at her without laughing.

But that wasn't Jack's only talent. He'd also turned out to be a great cardplayer. Maisie set up his cards on a little stand she made from some bookends so he could see them. She taught Jack all the basic games: war, go fish, old maid, rummy. They played for hours every night. Sometimes Jack won, sometimes Maisie did. But they never kept score. They just played for fun.

Maisie had never been happier.

Then one hot, sunny afternoon, Maisie had an idea. Mother and Father were both out, and none of the neighbors seemed to be home. With no one around, Maisie decided to play cards on the screened-in porch. It was shady and cool there. It was fun to play in a new place, especially because Jack was being so hilarious. He kept saying "go fish" in different voices. Every time Maisie asked if he had any aces, or tens, he'd answer, "Go fish," in the voice of Tess Twillingham or Miss Nancy. Maisie couldn't stop laughing. The tears were running down her face, and she could hardly breathe, but Jack wouldn't quit. He loved to see her laugh.

Jack and Maisie were so caught up in their game that they forgot to be careful. They did not remember to speak softly. And they didn't even notice when two shadowy figures paused to listen from behind the lilac bushes.

They didn't realize how easy it was to see through the screened windows.

They didn't know that their secret was out.

The Disappearing Dog

The next morning, Mother told Maisie she had a special surprise for her. "I've signed you up for a pottery class," she said. "Something to bring out your creative spark. You'll love it!"

Maisie wasn't very interested in pottery, and she felt that her creative spark was alive and well — after all, wasn't teaching a dog to talk pretty creative? Still, she knew there was no point in arguing with Mother.

"Your class doesn't begin until next week, but I thought we should go to the pottery studio today so you could meet the teacher. You can see what it's like," Mother said.

Maisie knew Mother always worried about how she would adjust to new things. She'd once heard Mother tell someone that she was a "sensitive child." Was that true? Maisie didn't think so, but it seemed that Mother's mind was made up.

"Can Jack walk downtown with us?" Maisie asked.

Mother sighed. "Let's leave him at home, okay? It's such a bother to have him along. We'd have to find a place to tie him up and all."

Maisie just shrugged. She should have known not to ask. Mother never liked taking walks with Jack. She went up to her room to change, and Jack followed her. "Sorry," she told him. "Do you want to stay inside or out while we're gone?"

"It's such a nice day," Jack answered, "I think I'd like to take a nap outside, under the apple tree."

So when Maisie and Mother left, they let Jack out into the yard and latched the gate of the picket fence behind them. "Bye, Jack," Maisie called. "Be a good dog."

Jack, naturally, did not reply. He knew enough to keep quiet when anyone else was around. But he gave Maisie a dog smile and a wag of his feathery tail. She even thought she saw him wink at her.

All the way downtown, Maisie thought about how lucky she was to have Jack. She had never realized how lonely she was before she had him. Jack had always been good company. Now he was *terrific* company.

Mother talked happily during their walk. She didn't seem to notice that Maisie was lost in thought. At the pottery studio, she embarrassed Maisie by asking all kinds of questions about the classes. Mother seemed especially worried about safety measures around the kiln, the hot oven where clay pots were hardened. The teacher answered her patiently. He even gave Maisie a secret little smile, which made Maisie like him.

Afterward, Mother asked Maisie if she'd like to have lunch downtown.

"No, thank you," Maisie said. "I told Jack I'd be home by noon."

Mother gave her an odd look. "Really, Maisie," she chuckled. "It's not as if the dog can tell time."

Actually, he could. Maisie had taught him.

But Maisie realized her mistake and corrected

herself. "I mean, Jack's been in the yard for a while. And he hasn't had a real walk yet today."

"He's just a dog," Mother said. "But I guess he's better company than your old mother." She sniffed and turned toward home without another word.

If only she knew, Maisie thought, following along.

"Jack!" she called out as they came up to the house. "I'm home!" She lifted the latch on the gate, expecting Jack to come running when he heard the hinges squeak. But he didn't. There was no blur of black fur, no eager face, and no panting, happy welcome home.

"Jack?" Maisie called, stepping around to the side yard to check under the apple tree. "Where are you?"

There was no answer.

Jack was gone.

■ ■ ■

"I knew it!" Oliver's voice filled Mr. Taylor's classroom. He was so excited that his glasses had slipped almost all the way down his nose. "I knew they were going to steal him!"

Molly looked frightened. Cricket stared at Oliver. "What do you mean?" she asked. "How do you know somebody stole him?"

Oliver was impatient. "Don't you remember? Somebody was watching and listening when Jack and Maisie were on the porch." He turned to Mr. Taylor. "Am I right?" he asked.

"I guess we'll find out," Mr. Taylor answered. He glanced up at the clock. "I think there's just enough time for a little more."

Where's Jack?

Maisie couldn't believe it. She walked all the way around the house, checking under every tree and between the shrubs. The only sign of Jack was a small circle of flattened grass under the apple tree.

Mother didn't seem too concerned. "He may have found a way inside," she suggested. Maisie's heart lifted. Maybe they'd left the back door ajar, or maybe Jack had figured out how to open the screen door. Maybe he was close by. He could be sitting inside with his tail thumping the floor as he waited for her.

Maisie pulled open the screen door. She stepped into the front hall and listened. The house seemed cool and dark after the heat of the sun. It was silent and still. Maisie waited for the familiar *click-click* of Jack's toenails as he trotted down the stairs. It didn't come. The house had never seemed so hushed.

Maisie ran back out onto the screened porch. When she saw the deck of cards she'd left on a table the day before, she burst into tears.

Mother joined her there. "He'll come back," she said, patting Maisie awkwardly on the shoulder.

Maisie knew Mother didn't really care whether Jack came back or not. Sure enough, the next thing she said was, "Well, why don't I go make us some lunch?" With that, she hurried off to the kitchen.

Maisie buried her face in her hands and tried to think. Where could Jack have gone? The gate had been latched when they came home. That meant one of three things. One: Jack had learned to let himself out and latch the gate behind him. Two: Jack had managed to jump the tall fence. Or three: Someone had opened the gate, come into the yard, kidnapped Jack, and left, closing the gate.

Maisie could hardly stand to think of number three.

Maisie thought for a moment. Jack was happy

with her. He'd told her so over and over. He thanked her many times for teaching him to talk, introducing him to go fish, and making sure Mother bought his favorite kind of dog food. Why would he leave on his own?

So that was it. Numbers one and two made no sense. Only number three did. Jack had been kidnapped.

Maisie started to cry again. Did somebody steal him just because he was such a handsome dog? Or did they know his secret?

Did somebody know Jack could talk?

Maisie saw a hint of movement outside. "Jack!" She jumped up to look out the window. But it wasn't Jack. It was Adam and Annie Ackerman, playing catch in front of their house.

Maisie ran to the door. "Adam!" she cried. "Annie!" She hurried down the porch stairs. "You haven't seen Jack, have you?"

Annie shook her head. But Adam smiled. "Sure," he answered. "He was napping under the apple tree this morning." He pointed to the spot.

Maisie didn't trust herself to speak for a moment.

"Well, he's gone now," she reported finally. "Did you see anyone come into the yard?"

Adam shrugged. "Nope. We can ask the others." He gave Maisie a sympathetic look. "He'll be back," he said. "Some dogs just like to roam around."

"Not Jack," Maisie said distractedly. "He always said home was best."

Annie's eyes widened. "You mean —" she began.

But Adam interrupted her. "He always said *what?*"

Maisie caught herself. She'd slipped again! "I mean, he's the kind of dog who likes to stay close to home, that's all." Without looking at Annie, she said good-bye and wandered back to the porch. Mother came out with a plate of tuna sandwiches, but Maisie wasn't hungry. She just sat and thought. How was she ever going to find Jack on her own? She didn't even know where to start.

Then she heard a tap at the screen door.

It was Adam and Annie, back again — and Alison and Arthur, too.

"I can't believe Jack is missing!" Alison said.

"Why would he run away?" Arthur added.

"We can help," Annie said. "I know what he looks like. Maybe we can put up signs."

Maisie felt like crying. Why were they being so nice to her? They weren't even her friends, and they never could be. Mother wouldn't allow it.

"I'll be okay," she said, sniffling a little. She could tell they wanted to come in, but she didn't open the screen door or invite them onto the porch. The last thing she needed right now was to hear Mother complaining about the horrible Ackerman children.

"Thanks," was all she could manage before she turned away and went back inside.

Jack's Tale

Jack was in trouble. Big trouble. How had it all begun? He thought back.

When Maisie had gone off with her mother, Jack had drifted into a nap under the apple tree. He had been having a delicious dream about a big slice of apple pie topped with a scoop of soft, dripping, vanilla ice cream. But when he woke, he knew right away that he wasn't alone. There were two men standing over him. And something about the way they smelled made Jack want to run.

He jumped to his feet. He had to escape! But the men were blocking his way.

"Where ya think yer going?" asked the one with the black scruffy stuff all over his face — Jack thought it was called a beard. The man's voice was as rough as the short hair on his chin.

"Come here, you dumb mutt," said the taller

one. He had light-colored hair and angry red spots on his forehead. Without wasting a second, he bent down and clipped a long heavy leash onto Jack's collar.

"Dumb! Ha! This dog ain't dumb, Gomer. That's the whole point!" said the first one. "We're gonna make a lotta money when we sell this hound to the circus." He did a heavy, stomping sort of a dance and let out a yell that made Jack nervous.

"Quiet, Tommy," said the tall one, looking around nervously. "What if somebody hears you?" He grabbed the leash and pulled.

Jack planted his paws in the soft green grass, trying to anchor himself in Maisie's yard. He couldn't leave. What would Maisie think if she came home and found him gone? What would she do? The last thing he wanted was to leave her. And the last people he wanted to be with were these two men. They smelled of danger, and they growled when they spoke.

The taller man yanked and pulled, but Jack wouldn't budge. Finally, the bearded one just reached down and picked Jack up. Jack wriggled and squirmed, but the man carried him across the yard and out the gate. He stopped next to a big white car parked on the street in front of Maisie's house. "Open the trunk, Gomer," he ordered. His voice made the hair on the back of Jack's neck stand up. Gomer opened the empty black space in the back of the car.

Jack looked at the yawning hole and squirmed even harder. He was scared. He had never, ever bitten anybody, but now he snaked his head around, hoping to find some skin he could nip. A snarl rose out of his throat. He'd never growled that way before, not in his whole life.

"Hey!" yelled Tommy. "This crazy dog is trying to bite me!" And with that, he dumped Jack into the trunk and slammed the top down hard.

The crash of metal on metal made Jack quiver. He barked once, twice, hoping that somebody might hear him. But the only response was a banging on the lid above him. Then he heard somebody shout, "Shut up, mutt!"

"Let's get outta here," Jack heard. There were footsteps, the sound of slamming car doors, and the noise and rumble of a motor starting. With a screech of tires, the car took off, throwing Jack hard against the back of the trunk.

It was cold. And it was dark. And it felt like there wasn't enough air. Jack whimpered. He tucked his tail over his nose and tried to curl up into the tightest, tiniest ball possible.

They drove for hours. Every bump threw Jack against the trunk walls until his body was bruised and sore. The trunk smelled awful; it stank of sweat and gasoline and old, rotten things. Jack longed for the familiar smells of home: the mouth-watering aroma of beef stew, the special scent of Maisie's deck of cards, the comforting smell of his own bed.

Would he ever smell those things again? There was no way he could escape from the metal prison. Maybe when the car finally stopped and the men opened the lid, Jack could leap out and run for his life.

But how would he know which way to run? How would he ever find Maisie?

■ ■ ■

Mr. Taylor leaned back in his chair. The room was completely quiet. Cricket could hardly stand it. Poor Jack! Poor Maisie!

"You can't stop now!" Jennifer said, breaking the silence. "What happens next? What are the men going to do with Jack?"

Just then, the bell rang. Usually, that was the signal for everyone to run for their cubbies and get ready to go home. But nobody moved a muscle. They all just sat there, staring at Mr. Taylor.

He reached up to turn out the beautiful lamp over his chair. The painted scene went dark. "You'll have to wait until tomorrow to find out. Try not to worry about it too much," he added. He looked at Molly, who was biting her lower lip. She seemed to be holding back tears. "Remember, it's just a story," he added gently.

The Cabin in the Woods

Just a story! Was it really? It sounded so real. Cricket could tell that Molly and some of the other kids thought so, too. Even though Cricket knew that everything was probably going to work out okay for Jack, it was still so awful. She couldn't stop thinking about Jack being stolen by those two men. She imagined how Maisie felt when she came home to find her dog missing.

"Are you *sure* everything is all right at school?" her mother asked at dinner that night. She reached out a hand to touch Cricket's forehead.

Cricket nodded and tried to explain a little about the story, but she couldn't tell it the way Mr. Taylor did. Anyway, she still didn't know how it ended!

On Wednesday morning at sharing time,

Jennifer begged Mr. Taylor to go on with the story.

Mr. Taylor stroked his mustache, deep in thought. "Not right now," he said. "We have a lot to do today. Ms. Buckley is waiting for you in the music room, and after that we have math and then spelling. If we concentrate and work hard, we'll have a little more time at the end of the afternoon."

For the rest of the day, Mr. Taylor's class was on its best behavior ever. Cricket had never seen everybody so focused on getting their work done. Even Jason waited his turn before yelling out answers during math, and for once Leo didn't dawdle when he took his turn at the computer.

At two o'clock sharp, Mr. Taylor told them to clean up their desks and head to the reading corner. "Good work. We have just enough time to find out what happens next," he said as he turned on the lamp and settled into his chair.

Then he took a deep breath, looked up at the ceiling for a moment, and went on with the story. "Jack drifted in and out of sleep as the car hurtled along," Mr. Taylor began.

Jack woke up suddenly when the car swerved and slowed down. The car was shaking and rattling and bouncing, and Jack was thrown from side to side with every bump and turn.

He felt like a tug toy in the jaws of the butcher's rottweiler. He was sore and scared. *Let it stop, oh, please, let it stop!* Jack thought as he banged around inside the trunk.

Finally, the car came to a screeching halt. There was a moment of silence when the engine died, and Jack could hear a ringing in his ears. Then car doors slammed again.

"We're back!" he heard Tommy roar. "And wait'll you see what we brought!"

Footsteps stomped around to the back of the car. The lid was pulled open. By the time Jack remembered his plan to escape it was too late. He had meant to run away as soon as he could get free. But before he could move a single aching muscle, Tommy reached in to grab hold of his collar.

"Let's go," Tommy commanded.

Jack raised his head and looked at the man. He

was too sore to move. Behind Tommy's head, Jack saw tall trees against a dark, starry sky. There were new smells in the air, smells of smoke and of pine. The pine smell reminded Jack of the trees lining the creek where Maisie took him to wade on hot summer days.

"Come on! Hup! Jump outta there!" Tommy shouted.

Jack moved one paw and pushed himself to standing. His legs shook beneath him. His empty stomach growled for food.

"Faster!" yelled the man. "Oh, never mind. Take him outta there, Gomer."

Jack could tell by the way he smelled that Tommy was afraid of being bitten. Good. The other man, Gomer, wasn't as rough. Gomer reached in and pulled Jack out of the trunk, cradling him in his arms. He lurched up a path that led to a squat, dark shape. Jack peered into the night. The shape was a house, but it was not like Maisie's nice, big house. It had light spilling out of the windows, but it did not look welcoming. It did not look like home.

There were more men standing outside the house — three more. They were all as rough and frightening as the two who had grabbed Jack from his peaceful, grassy napping place.

"Whatcha got there, Tommy?" bellowed one of them, a man with a stomach so big Jack wondered how he could stand up straight.

"Is that a *dog*?" yelled another. "Are you crazy? We don't need any pets to take care of."

"This ain't no ordinary dog," Tommy told them. "In fact, this ain't a dog at all. Muttley here is a gold mine."

The men looked at Jack, who was trembling in Gomer's arms.

"Gold mine?" asked the fat man. He started to laugh. "That pooch ain't worth a penny! What, is it some kinda show dog or something?"

"You could say that," Tommy answered. He faced the others. "This dog can talk."

Now they were all laughing. "Sure," said one of them. "Right. And my mother's the queen of France."

"Say something, Muttley," Tommy ordered Jack. "Show them how you talk."

Jack was silent.

"Now!" Tommy took a step toward Gomer, who was still holding Jack.

Jack shrank back. He felt Gomer flinch, too.

"C'mon, you stupid mutt. Talk like you did yesterday." Tommy's face was right up next to Jack's. He was close enough that Jack could smell onions, and cheese, and tobacco.

Jack turned his head away and did not let out even the smallest growl. He wanted to disappear. He wanted something to eat. He wanted to go to sleep.

He wanted Maisie.

Tommy ordered Gomer to put Jack down. Then Tommy stood, staring down at Jack, commanding him to speak. Over and over, he yelled at the cowering dog.

Finally, Jack had had enough.

He barked.

There was a burst of mean laughter from the men. "Nice talking," said the fat man.

"Stupid mutt," Tommy snarled. He turned to the men. "Never mind. I'm hungry. We'll show you tomorrow. Then you'll be sorry you laughed. This dog's gonna make us all rich, and don't you forget it."

Gomer picked up Jack's leash and dragged him up the rocky path to the house. "Go lie down in the corner," he told him once they were inside the small, dark cabin. Jack slunk over to a dark place near a big, old chair. The house smelled a lot like the trunk of the car. Except for one thing: There was the smell of meat sizzling in a pan on the stove. Jack couldn't help drooling when the smell hit his nose.

"Maybe we should feed him," Gomer suggested. "He looks hungry."

"Sure," Tommy agreed. "The dog's no good to us if he starves to death."

It was the first good thing Jack had heard. He could almost taste the meat in his mouth.

"Give him that stuff on the counter," Tommy told Gomer.

Gomer scraped a pile of vegetable peelings, a

moldy piece of bread, and an apple core into a bowl and put it down in front of Jack. "Sorry, pooch," he whispered.

Jack's stomach turned when he smelled the mold. But he was too hungry to turn away. He ate the pile of garbage as fast as he could. Then he stretched, limped around in a circle three times, and curled his aching body into a small, tight ball on the hard floor.

Aces High

A shout rang out, and Jack woke up. For one quick second he thought he was at Maisie's house.

Then he smelled the men.

It all came flooding back. Cautiously, Jack opened one eye and looked around. The five men were sitting around a round table near the stove. The room was dark except for a sputtering lantern in the middle of the table. Rings of smoke hung over the men as they puffed on fat, stinky cigars. They smelled like the ones Mr. Rispoli chewed on while he swept the sidewalk in front of his hardware store. Once, Jack had sniffed at Mr. Rispoli's cigar butt because he thought it was a piece of food. Once had been enough.

The shouting had stopped, and now the men were quiet. Jack watched again as Tommy's big hands made quick motions toward each of them in turn. *Slip, slap.* Jack's ears pricked forward at the familiar sound. He'd know that noise anywhere.

Tommy was dealing cards.

"Queen of hearts to Brucie," Tommy announced, describing the hands he was dealing. "No help with the straight. And a two to Harvey. That makes a pair. Could be something there, unless — oops, Gomer's got a pair of eights now. That beats a pair of deuces."

It didn't sound like they were playing go fish. But the names of the cards were the same. And hearing them made Jack yearn for Maisie. He thought of her. She was probably sitting alone in her room, playing solitaire. Or maybe she wasn't playing cards at all. Maybe she was just gazing out the window into the darkness, watching and waiting for Jack to return. He had to get back to her. He had to.

Without a sound, he crept closer to the table. Maybe if he watched the men closely, he could figure out how to escape.

There was the clink of coins and the murmur of

"I'll see you fifty and raise you a dollar." More cards slip-slapped onto the table. More coins clinked.

"Show 'em, gentlemen," Tommy said.

Another roar rang out. "A royal flush!" Gomer yelled. "And you with that poker face. Why, Van, you old faker. I thought I had you beat with my full house."

Poker! Jack had heard of the game, but he and Maisie had never played it. Curious, he moved even closer, until he was tucked under the table near Gomer's feet. And he watched, and he listened, and he learned.

The men played on, through the night. While they played, they told one another stories. They told tall tales about the pioneers and lumberjacks who'd tamed the wild land a hundred years ago. They told of men who could clear acres of forest with a single swing of an ax or drink a river in one gulp, and of women who could shoot the head off a match at fifty paces. Finally, Jack could hear their voices blurring as they grew tired.

But Jack had never felt more awake in his life.

He had come up with an idea, and there was no time to waste. They might stop the stories and card-playing any minute and go to bed. The sun might rise and shine through the windows to reveal Jack's hiding place under the table.

Tommy had just dealt another hand of poker, calling out each card as he laid it down. Jack was listening so closely that he could hear the men arranging their cards. He recognized the sounds of them slipping cards in and out to put them in order and figure out what treasures they held. They made bets. They turned in some of their cards — one for Gomer, three for Harvey, two each for Van, Brucie, and Tommy — and got new ones. Bet again. Then Tommy said to "show 'em."

"Four aces!" crowed Gomer. "Read 'em and weep!"

This was Jack's big chance. He didn't have a moment to lose, and he knew it. In the silence after the men shouted in disbelief, he spoke up from beneath the table. "Four aces, my eye," he said gruffly, in a perfect imitation of Tommy's low voice. "I saw you slip that ace of hearts into your sleeve after your last deal." Jack held his breath, hoping that it was dark enough so that the other men would believe Tommy was the one who had spoken.

"What did you say, Tommy?" Gomer sounded stunned. "Are you accusing me of cheating?"

It had worked! Jack didn't miss a beat. "You bet I am," he growled before Tommy could deny it. "What do you take me for, a fool? You're the worst poker player in four states. Cheating is the only way you can win."

"Wait," said the real Tommy. "Who's saying that? It's not —" But Brucie interrupted.

"I bet Tommy's right!" Brucie said. "Now that I think of it, I heard talk of Gomer being a big swindler."

Gomer gasped. But before he could defend himself, Jack spoke up.

"You're just jealous," Jack responded quickly, in Gomer's voice. "You're so dumb you couldn't win even *if* you cheated."

Jack jumped as a loud crashing thundered over his head. Someone was pounding on the table.

"Dumb?" Brucie roared. "I'll tell you what's dumb. Hanging out with a bunch of losers like you is dumb."

"But Brucie, I didn't say you were —" Gomer began.

But it was too late. Jack had stirred up everyone's feelings.

All five chairs scraped back at once. The men jumped to their feet and began to fling their fists at one another. Jack heard grunts of pain as the men swore and shouted and stomped and kicked.

Jack slipped out from under the table, dodging flying chairs. Silently, he crawled along the wall toward the front door. He pushed his nose against it. The door didn't budge. Behind him, the shouts grew louder. He pushed again harder, using the last of his strength.

Still the door didn't open.

Then Jack heard footsteps behind him. He turned to look fearfully over his shoulder. After all that, his plan had failed. His chance to escape was gone.

But it was Gomer, staggering away from the

fighting. "Good idea, Muttley," he said. "Let's get out of here." He turned the doorknob and pushed open the door.

With one quick, grateful glance at Gomer, Jack dashed out and ran as fast as he could. He headed straight for the woods. As soon as he was out of sight of the cabin, he stopped. He stood still for a moment and gobbled up huge lungfuls of the clear, cold night air.

■ ■ ■

Mr. Taylor stopped and took a deep breath himself.

The room was completely quiet for a moment. Then everybody started talking at once.

Oliver burst out with a cheer. "Yay, Jack!" he yelled.

"Did you hear him talk about my card during the game?" asked Jason.

"That was so cool!" Jennifer said. "Your ace of hearts!"

"Those guys were scary," Molly said. "I'm glad Jack got away."

Mr. Taylor nodded. "This is a good stopping

point," he said. "At least you know he's safe —
for now."

For now? Cricket wondered what he meant by
that. But it was time to head home. She knew she
would find out more the next day.

Maisie

On Thursday morning Cricket got to school a little early. Since it was raining, nobody was outside playing kickball. She headed into her classroom. Mr. Taylor was busy at his desk, but he smiled and waved when he saw her come in. Jennifer and Jason were early, too. They were sitting by the window. Jason was shuffling a deck of cards in the special way he'd learned from his grandfather. Nobody else could do it, but Jason was really good at it.

"Hey!" Cricket asked Jason. "Aren't those your Garfield cards? What about your missing ace?"

Jason smiled. "Found it! It was in my math book. I was using it as a bookmark. Want to play rummy?" he asked, starting to deal three hands without even waiting for her answer.

First her tennis ball, and then Jason's ace of

hearts. The lost things were starting to turn up! Cricket turned to look at Mr. Taylor. Was he making it happen, somehow?

That afternoon, Mr. Taylor didn't have to tell them when it was time to clean up their desks. By two o'clock sharp the whole class was gathered in the reading corner. They waited for him to switch on the light, sit down, and go on with the story.

"Let's see," said Mr. Taylor, rubbing his long hands together once he'd folded himself into the chair. "Where were we?" He put his hands on his bony knees.

"Jack got away from the mean men!" Jennifer offered.

"He tricked them," added Jason. "By talking."

Cricket raised her hand and waited until Mr. Taylor looked at her. "But now he has to get back to Maisie."

"Maisie," Mr. Taylor repeated. "Exactly. He has to get back to Maisie. How do you think Maisie is feeling these days?"

"Really, really sad," Leo said quietly, staring down at the floor.

Cricket could tell he was thinking about Tracker.

"That's right," said Mr. Taylor. "Maisie *was* really sad."

...

Back in Tinsdale, Maisie sat near the window of her room. She was too miserable to sleep and too upset to read. She missed Jack so much! Every time she looked at his bed she started to cry.

Where could he be? She had looked everywhere in town. She had walked up and down the streets calling him. She had gone to the police and described Jack in case anyone reported a missing dog. She couldn't think of anything else to do. Mother and Father were no help. Father seemed bored by the whole situation, and Mother just kept saying, "He'll find his way home eventually."

But what if he couldn't? Maisie knew that if Jack had been kidnapped he might be far, far away by now. And if the people who took him knew he could talk, who knew what they were making him do? Maisie pictured Jack in a sideshow at a carnival, forced to say ridiculous things while people stared and laughed.

She cried herself to sleep that night. The next morning, when she was sitting on the porch playing a listless game of clock solitaire, she heard a knock at the screen door. Maisie looked up to see Alison's smiling face. She was standing on the steps again, with Andrew, Aaron, and Annie.

Alison was holding a big pile of cardboard, and Annie gripped a handful of crayons. "It's us again," Alison said cheerfully.

"We'll help you make some signs," Aaron said. "Adam and Arthur are out searching the neighborhood for clues. Don't worry, we'll find him."

Maisie glanced over her shoulder. What would Mother say if she let this crowd of Ackermans onto the porch? Then she thought of Jack. Poor Jack, out there in the world somewhere without her.

She needed help finding him.

She needed friends.

She swung the screen door wide open.

"Come on in," she said.

The morning flew by as they worked on their signs. The Ackermans asked Maisie for every detail about Jack's appearance and habits so that people would know him if they saw him. It almost made Maisie cry again to describe the way one of Jack's ears stood up while the other flopped over, but it was also nice to be able to talk about him. She told them everything she could think of.

Well, almost everything. There was one tiny little fact she neglected to mention.

■ ■ ■

Hands went up all around the circle. Mr. Taylor smiled and leaned back in his chair.

"I know what it is!" yelled three voices at once.

"She didn't tell them Jack can talk!" Jason shouted.

Mr. Taylor waited for everyone to settle down. "One at a time," he suggested. "That way we can all hear what you have to say."

"Jason's right," Oliver said. "I bet she didn't tell them he can play cards, either."

Jennifer nodded. "I wouldn't tell, if I was her. Nobody would believe her, anyway."

"Will they find him?" asked Leo. For the first

time all day he wasn't drooping over, looking at the floor. For the first time all day he was thinking about something besides Tracker being gone.

Molly raised her hand. "What happens next?" she asked when Mr. Taylor nodded in her direction. "I mean, what happens to Jack? And what about the boat? When does Oliver's boat come into the story?" Cricket was amazed. Molly had become a regular chatterbox.

Cricket raised her hand, too. "Is Jack going to get back to Maisie?" she asked.

"Let's find out," suggested Mr. Taylor. "So, when we left Jack, he had just escaped from the cabin in the woods, right?"

"Right!" everybody yelled.

And Mr. Taylor went on with the story.

Jack on the Run

Once *he had gotten the smell of men and cigars* out of his nose, Jack was ready to move. He headed toward the rising sun because it gave him something to aim for. He knew he was far, far away from Maisie. The car had brought him a long way, much faster than he could go by foot. Walking, it would take him days to get home. But if he chose the right direction and if he kept going, he would get there. He knew Maisie was waiting. He had to find his way home somehow.

Jack set off at a steady trot. He was still stiff and sore from his time in the trunk, but his muscles warmed up as he moved. He wove through thick underbrush and squished through soggy mud. He frightened fat birds from their nests and saw bushy-tailed gray squirrels scramble up trees as he passed.

As the sun rose higher, Jack began to pant. Finally, when the sun was directly overhead, he scraped out a shallow pit in the cool dirt beneath a tangle of prickly bushes, and he lay down for a rest.

When he woke up, the sun was no longer a bright hot disk overhead. It was big and red and it was just disappearing behind the far-off hills. Long shadows lay across the forest floor. Jack was so hungry and thirsty that he felt dizzy. He knew he had to move on if he hoped to find food and water. It was cooler now, and the woods weren't as thick. Jack moved quickly through the twilight. When he came to an open field, he trotted across it, watching warily for any movement that might signal danger.

Jack didn't find food that night. But he did not stop. He trotted onward, across fields and through towering pine forests, as a silvery half-moon rose and set. He saw owls swooping after their prey and eyes glowing red in the dark. The night was alive — and Jack was dead tired.

Still, he did not stop. He kept moving as the sun rose and set, rose and set.

Finally, one morning, just as the sun began to

rise, Jack froze and lifted his head. He sniffed, and sniffed again. Oh, what a wonderful smell!

It was the river.

The smell of mud and fish and moving water all combined in just a particular way. Jack had no doubt: This was the very same river that flowed past Tinsdale. Past Maisie's town. Past home.

How many days had it been since he lay in the yard under the apple tree? Four? Five? Too many.

He galloped toward the smell, forgetting his exhaustion and his grumbling belly. He came out into an open, grassy space that rolled down and away. In the distance, he could see the wide, flowing ribbon of familiar brownish water. He wanted to run straight into it, thrust his nose deep down, and drink until he couldn't drink any more.

"Doggy!" he heard.

And then he smelled something else. People. And food. Jack slowed down to sniff the scent of bacon, his favorite Sunday morning treat at Maisie's.

"Daddy! Look! Doggy!"

At the edge of the clearing, a little girl stood in the doorway of a small, tidy white cottage. She was pointing at him and laughing happily, her blue eyes squeezed nearly shut by her plump pink cheeks. A man stood close to her, aiming a spray of water at a bed of purple flowers.

He turned to look at Jack.

"Scram!" he said. "Get out of here!" He pointed the hose at Jack.

"No, Daddy!" shrieked the little girl. "Want doggy! Want doggy!" Her mouth turned down and she began to screech. The high-pitched noise hurt Jack's ears and made him whimper.

"Amanda, sweetie!" the man said. "The doggy is all dirty. He's probably sick. He might bite us. The doggy can't stay."

A woman came to the door and stared at Jack. "Ugh!" she cried. "Look at that ugly stray. His fur is all matted and full of burrs. Get rid of him, Phillip."

"No! No! NO-NO-NO-NO-NO!!!!" screamed the little girl. "Want doggy. Want doggy! WANT DOGGY!"

The man and the woman stared helplessly at their little girl.

"Well," said the man when the girl paused for a breath. "I suppose if I gave him a bath . . ."

An hour later, Jack lay on a soft, warm bed made of clean towels. The bed sat in a patch of sunshine on the screened porch. Jack was clean and sweet-smelling, his belly was full almost to bursting, and the only sound was the comforting rhythm of the mother reading a story to her little girl.

Amanda sat next to Jack. She stroked his silky ears as she listened. "Good doggy," she murmured, leaning down to kiss his muzzle. The golden heart she wore on a chain around her neck bumped against his nose.

■ ■ ■

Jennifer jumped up. "Guess what!" she said. "I found my locket last night. It was under my bed." She pulled it out from beneath her sweater. "Want to see the pictures inside?" She undid the clasp and handed it to Mr. Taylor.

"Very nice, Jennifer," he said. Cricket couldn't believe her ears. First of all, why wasn't Mr. Taylor mad at Jennifer for interrupting? And second, how could he say "very nice" about those dumb baby pictures?

"Shall we pass it around?" he asked. When Jennifer nodded, Mr. Taylor handed the locket to Oliver. Then he leaned back in his chair.

Cricket let out a sigh of relief. He was going to tell more of the story.

■ ■ ■

Jack felt Amanda's locket bump his nose many, many times over the following days. The little girl never seemed to get tired of patting and kissing him. Her parents fed him well and let him sleep in her room. The days passed in a blur as he napped and ate, getting stronger every day for his trip back to Maisie.

When he was awake, he lay resting for hours with his head on Amanda's lap while her parents told her story after story. The stories were about princesses and ducklings and happy pigs, fairies and elves and friendly giants. Jack liked the stories. He liked Amanda's parents. And he liked Amanda, as long as she wasn't crying. He even kind of liked his new name, Silky.

But all the time, Jack knew he would not stay with them forever. He would only stay as long as it took him to get ready. Ready to find his way home.

One afternoon when Amanda was napping, Jack lay on the porch near the swing, where the man and woman sat talking. Their voices were a soft murmur.

"It's time to pack up," said the woman. "We have to leave the day after tomorrow. It's a long drive back home."

"I hate to go back to the city," the man said, stretching and yawning.

"I know. We've been so happy here. Especially since Silky turned up. Amanda hasn't had a single tantrum since he's been with us."

Jack cocked an ear toward them when he heard his name. He was a little sorry to hear that they were leaving. But he knew it was time for him to leave, too. Time to find his way back to Maisie.

"I hope he'll like the city," the man said.

"He'll have to," answered the woman. "Amanda will never give up Silky now."

Jack Saves His Own Skin

Jack's heart began thumping fast. *He did not* want to live in a city with this family, no matter how nice they were. He belonged to Maisie. And his best chance for finding his way back to her was to follow the river that flowed near this house. If these people took him away from the river, he might never get home!

Once again, Jack knew he had to escape. Could he run for it? Not this time. The family kept him inside or on a leash at all times. He had to come up with another idea. Could he use his secret talent again?

That evening, after supper, Jack walked into the kitchen while the woman was washing dishes.

"I'll be done in a minute, honey," she said, without turning around. "Then I'll help you put the rack on the car."

The woman thought Jack was her husband! He thought fast. "Fine," he answered, in the man's voice. "Listen, darling, I've been thinking. Maybe Silky wouldn't be so happy in the city. Maybe it's selfish to take him with us."

The woman stopped scrubbing the plate she was holding, but she didn't turn around. "Well," she said thoughtfully.

Jack decided to quit while he was ahead. "Just something to think about," he said as he tiptoed out of the kitchen. He knew he still had to change the minds of two other people.

Later that night, Amanda had a bad dream. Her father slept right through her cries, but her mother went to comfort her. While the mother was gone, Jack crept into the parents' darkened bedroom. He gave the father's back a little shove with his nose.

"Hmmph?" asked the man, waking up only halfway. "What is it?"

"It's just," Jack said, in the woman's voice, "I've been thinking. Isn't a dog an awful lot of responsibility? We're both so busy when we're back in the city. Maybe Silky would be happier staying here, in the country. I'm sure we could find him a good home."

"Hmpph," the man mumbled.

Jack slipped out of the room just as Amanda's mother returned.

When Amanda woke up, early the next morning, Jack was waiting next to her crib. "Does Amanda want a kitty?" he asked, in a coaxing voice. "Soft kitty, nice kitty. Amanda wants kitty. No dog, kitty."

Amanda stared at him, spellbound.

There was a moment of silence. Then she began to shriek.

Her parents came running. "What is it, darling? What's the matter? What does Amanda want?" her mother asked, scooping her up.

"Want kitty!" Amanda cried. "Nice kitty! No dog! Kitty!"

Jack saw her parents exchange a look. "You know," said Amanda's mother, "I've been thinking."

"So have I," said Amanda's father.

And later that morning, Amanda's father clipped a leash to Jack's collar and led him down to the general store on the banks of the river. Jack was surprised. He'd expected to be set free to wander as a stray again. But Amanda's father insisted that he needed a good home.

"Know anybody who's looking for a dog?" he asked the shopkeeper.

"As a matter of fact, I do," she replied. "Go see Captain Andy, down at the docks."

Captain Andy was a barrel-chested man with a red face and a loud voice. He reached down to thump Jack's sides. Jack liked the feel of the man's big hands patting him. "This one's a beaut, he is!" he cried. "Are you sure he's not spoken for?"

"He's a stray," said Amanda's father. "But he's a sweet dog. Smart, too. We'd love to keep him, but we just can't."

"He'll make a good river dog," Captain Andy said, rubbing Jack's ears. "I've been looking for a pup ever since Bowser fell off my boat and drowned."

Jack shivered.

He had never been much of a swimmer. He liked to wade in the creek or even dip his toes into the river, but Maisie had never been able to convince him that it would be fun to plunge in and swim against the current to fetch a ball.

Now, like it or not, Jack was going to be a river dog.

■ ■ ■

"My boat!" Oliver cried. "I knew it had to be coming soon. I bet Jack is going to love being on a boat."

Just then, the final bell rang. "That's it for today," Mr. Taylor said. "We'll finish up tomorrow."

Everybody groaned as Mr. Taylor reached up and turned off the lamp. It was the first time Cricket was ever sorry to see school end. She couldn't believe Jack's story would be over tomorrow.

After school, Cricket was supposed to go over to Oliver's. He was going to show her a model airplane he was working on. She didn't care too much about model airplanes, but she liked going to Oliver's. There were usually good cookies at his house, and Sophie was fun to play with — as long as she wasn't screaming. You could always make her laugh if you made the right face.

"Why have you been acting so weird all week? You're so quiet." Oliver asked as they started walking toward his house.

Cricket shrugged. She was too embarrassed to tell him about Steps One through Five. Oliver would think it was silly to worry about things like Raising Your Hand or Waiting Your Turn. Anyway, being Kathryn wasn't working very well so far. Mr. Taylor didn't seem impressed by her good classroom manners. He didn't seem impressed by her at all. She had to try harder.

She changed the subject to Mr. Taylor's story, and they talked about Maisie and Jack, and how he was going to find his way home, and what it would be like to have a talking dog. Once they got to Oliver's, they had a snack. Then they went down to the basement so Oliver could show Cricket his model. It was pretty cool after all. Cricket let Oliver tell her the name of every single part.

"And we're going to paint it, and put on decals and everything," Oliver told her. He looked up at the shelf above the workbench. "Where's that paint?"

Cricket looked, too. "Is it in that box?" she asked, pointing to a big, dusty cardboard carton.

Oliver climbed up onto the workbench to pull the box down. "Hey," he said. "I remember this." He turned it around so Cricket could see some writing on the side. TOYS FOR BABY BROTHER, it said. "I made Mom write that when we put this stuff away," he said. "That was back when I was hoping Sophie was going to be a boy." He opened the box and rummaged around inside. Then he started laughing.

"What?" Cricket asked.

Oliver pulled a toy boat out of the box and held it up. "Found it!" he said.

Life on the River

The next morning, Cricket raised her hand at sharing time. "Oliver found his boat!" she said when Mr. Taylor called on her. She hoped she sounded happy and excited so the teacher wouldn't worry about her and phone her mother again.

"That's wonderful," he said. "Glad to hear it. Maybe Oliver would like to tell us more about it?"

Suddenly, Cricket felt ashamed. She should have let Oliver tell about finding the boat. She looked down at the floor, hardly listening as Oliver explained about the box of old toys. She couldn't get anything right. She wasn't a good Kathryn at all.

When Oliver had finished, Mr. Taylor asked if anybody else had anything to share.

"I just want to know what happened to Jack," said Jennifer.

Molly raised her hand. "Me, too," she said.

Mr. Taylor smiled. "We'll finish up the story this afternoon," he promised.

They all worked hard that day. When the two o'clock bell rang, everybody cheered and ran for the reading corner.

Mr. Taylor turned on the lamp and settled into his chair. "So, where were we?" he asked.

"Jack is going on the boat with Captain Andy!" yelled Oliver.

Mr. Taylor nodded. "Of course," he said. "The boat."

■ ■ ■

Captain Andy waved as Amanda's father walked off. He looked down at Jack. "Oops," he said. "Forgot to ask your name. Oh, well. I'll call you Blackie. That ought to do."

Jack had to be coaxed onto the gangplank that led to Captain Andy's towboat.

His legs shook a little as he stepped off solid ground and onto the narrow walkway. He didn't like the way the gangplank bounced, and he didn't like the muddy brown water moving beneath him. It made him dizzy.

"Come on, there, boy," said Captain Andy patiently. "You can do it." He put a hand on Jack's side and steadied him. After a step or two, Jack decided to run the rest of the way onto the wide, open deck of the boat. "That's it!" said Captain Andy. "We'll make a towboat dog of you yet."

Jack made his way over to the middle of the boat. The footing felt steadier there, and the water was farther away. He curled up on a pile of rope and watched the crew closely.

"Cast off, now! Heading downriver, boys!" cried the captain as they started to move. "We'll pick up a fleet of barges south of Tinsdale."

Jack leaped to his feet. Tinsdale! His ears pricked up and he began to sniff the air, hoping for some small scent of home.

"Look, Blackie likes being on a boat!" said one of the crew. "His tail is wagging."

After a day or two, Jack decided that life on the river was not so bad. The men worked hard all day, but late in the afternoon Captain Andy searched out a place for the boat to rest. "Let's stop for the night!" he shouted out. "Tie up at the dock on the starboard bank!" Once they tied up, the crew had time to relax. After sharing their hearty meal with Jack, they headed for the deck. Leaning against piles of rope, they gazed at the stars. After a while, one of them began to tell a tale of life on the river. Another man picked up the story and added to it with a yarn about adventure on the high seas. Jack lay nearby, listening happily to tales of wild storms and becalmed ships, of pirates and swindlers, of tropical paradises and haunted river islands.

Jack loved the stories. Even more, he loved knowing that each day of travel brought him closer to Maisie. He would have been completely happy, if only Captain Andy would stop talking about swimming lessons for him. Jack knew he would never get completely used to the murky brown water rushing past the sides of the boat.

On the third day, when the sun was low in the sky and the river was a wide ribbon of pink and gold,

Jack suddenly caught a whiff of something familiar. He ran to the bow of the boat and stood stiff-legged and quivering, his nose high in the air as he took in great lungfuls. Home! They were so close he could practically smell the roses in Maisie's yard.

"Are we tying up at Tinsdale, Cap'n?" he heard one of the men ask.

Jack turned to look at Captain Andy just in time to catch him shaking his head. "Not this trip," he said. "We've got to make up some time. We may have to keep moving all night." He shook his head tiredly and headed belowdecks.

Jack couldn't believe his ears. Not stop? How would he get back to Maisie? He stared at the water, wondering if he could leap off the boat and swim to shore as they passed Tinsdale. But the current was so strong, and the water was so dark. What if he drowned like Bowser? For a moment, he wished Captain Andy had given him those swimming lessons after all.

There had to be another solution. But there was no time to think! Through the dusk, he could see the wharves of Tinsdale sliding into sight. Suddenly,

Jack let out a yell. "Tie up for the night, boys! Mooring on the starboard side!" he hollered, imitating Captain Andy's roar.

He felt a little bad about tricking the crew since they'd all been so nice to him. But he *had* to get back to Maisie, and this might be his only chance.

There was a moment of confusion as the men wondered why "Cap'n" had changed his mind. But as always, they obeyed orders. Before Captain Andy could emerge from belowdecks, the boat had steered to the right and the crew had tossed ropes to men waiting on the wharf.

"What's this?" Captain Andy said, rushing up onto the deck. "Why are we tying up? Blackie! Hey! Where are you going?"

But Jack didn't hear him. He leaped off the boat the moment it was close enough to the dock. Breathlessly, he galloped up the long hill that rose from the river. He was running as fast as he could toward home, toward Maisie.

He didn't even see the pack of dogs come out from behind a warehouse. He didn't hear their growls.

Chased!

Grrab him!" *the leader of the pack snarled.* "Rrrun him out of ourrr town!"

The other dogs barked furiously as they chased the stranger down.

Their frenzied yelps finally reached Jack's ears. He slowed for a moment to look over his shoulder.

The dogs were closing in.

Jack knew there was a pack of wild dogs that roamed the riverbank. He had been gone for almost two weeks, and now it seemed as if the wild ones had claimed Tinsdale as their own. The leader was a long-legged dog with ratty brown fur and gleaming yellow eyes. He bore down on Jack and shouted at him in dog language.

"Go away! Rrrun! You don't belong here!"

Jack stopped in his tracks and turned to face the

leader. "I won't go!" he barked. "This is my place."
It felt strange to speak his own language again. It
had been a long time.

The lead dog roared, showing sharp white teeth
and a slavering red tongue. "Not anymorrre!" he
said. His foul breath filled Jack's nostrils. "Rrun
for your life!"

Jack ran.

With the pack chasing close behind him, he ran
all the way up the hill, past the butcher shop, past
the hardware store, past the Wilsons' house, and
past his own. "Oh, Maisie!" he thought as he galloped for his life. The picket fence around her
house was nothing but a blur as he raced by.

The pack ran and ran after him, chasing him far
out of town and deep into the forest. Night had
fallen, and the underbrush was thick. All the dogs
were exhausted. Their pace slowed as they stum-
bled through the pitch-dark woods. Even the lead
dog had stopped barking orders, but they were still
close behind Jack.

Suddenly, Jack tripped, banging his head on a
stone ledge. He slipped sideways — and disappeared

into a small, hidden cave. It was nothing more than a thin space between two high walls of mossy stone, but it was enough. Enough to hide Jack and his scent from the pack of wild dogs.

Jack squirmed even farther into the hole, amazed at his luck. He watched as the pack wandered into the clearing nearby, sniffing tiredly as the leader urged them on.

Finally, they all gave up and flopped down to rest. Almost instantly, their panting slowed as the dogs sank into sleep.

In his cool, hidden cave, Jack also slept. He knew he had to rest before he could escape and find his way back to Tinsdale.

He woke hours later to the light of a full, yellow moon streaming into the opening of the cave.

Out in the clearing, the wild dogs were stirring. Jack peered out to see them stretching and scratching in the moonlight. Jack saw a big black dog, a tiny shaggy dog who had once been white, and a spotted dog who used to live on Maisie's street. Tracker, that was her name. Tracker looked skinny and tired, and her tail hung down sadly.

■ ■ ■

Cricket pulled her eyes away from Mr. Taylor to look over at Leo. He was sitting up straight, staring into the distance. "Tracker," he whispered.

For the first time in a long time, Leo looked hopeful. Cricket knew that having Tracker in the story wasn't nearly as good as having her come home, but it was something.

Mr. Taylor met Leo's eyes and nodded. Then he went on.

■ ■ ■

Altogether, there were almost a dozen dogs. And then there was the leader.

He sat watching his pack. His yellow eyes glinted in the moonlight. "All rright," he said. "It's time to finish our task. We must find the stranger and rrun him to the edge of our lands so that he'll never come back."

"We're too tired!" whined the little dog.

"Let us rest some more," begged the black one.

The leader thought for a moment. He looked as

exhausted as the rest of them. "All rright," he agreed. "The night is long."

"Tell us a story," pleaded a dog with matted yellow hair. "Tell us a story while we rest."

The leader nodded. He sat back on his haunches and gazed up at the moon. And then he began. He told stories of wild beasts in the forest and strange monsters in the mountains, of animals no man or dog has ever seen.

Jack listened. And he waited. If he was lucky, he could escape before the sun came up and revealed his hiding place. But the leader's stories were so exciting that his pack stayed awake and on guard all night long.

Finally, the woods around them began to come into focus as the sky above turned from black to gray to golden. Dawn was breaking.

Jack put his head down and whimpered softly into the dirt on the floor of his cave. He could not imagine how he was going to escape this time. It had been such a long time since he'd curled up on his soft bed. And now he was starting to think he would never sleep there again. What if he never saw Maisie, never smelled her scent when he woke in the morning, never trotted next to her as they walked downtown?

And what would Maisie do without him? She would be so lonely, just sitting up in her room gazing out the window or playing solitaire.

Suddenly, Jack bolted to his feet. He wasn't ready to give up. He had managed to find a way out of every other fix he'd been in since he left home. He was sure he could come up with a way out of this one, too.

Home Again

Now, *Jack was tired of talking. He knew that* being able to speak English had helped him out of a few scrapes, but it was also what had gotten him into trouble in the first place. He decided, right then and there in that cave, that he was pretty much done with talking. All he wanted was the chance to go back to being a regular dog. He just wanted to sniff trees and take naps and bark at squirrels. No more imitating people.

But he knew he had to use what Maisie had taught him one last time, if it could help him get safely back to her. Silently, carefully, Jack crawled out of the cave and into a nearby thicket. He took a deep breath. Then he started talking.

"We'll find those wild dogs if we have to hunt all day," he said in a deep, gruff voice like Tommy's.

He watched as the leader of the pack stood up, his ears perked and his head cocked to listen.

"Find 'em," Jack answered himself, in a voice like Captain Andy's, "and shoot 'em."

"Can't have wild dogs running all over the place," he added in Gomer's voice. "Scaring children, chasing people's cats . . ."

The pack of dogs was stirring now, pacing as they whined and peered into the bushes. They watched their leader closely. All dogs understand human speech. The things they were hearing made them nervous.

Jack thought it might work.

"It's a trick," the yellow-eyed dog growled. "Steady, now." He braced himself and listened.

"My rifle's loaded," Jack finished, in Tommy's snarl. "We'll take care of those dogs."

That did it. The dogs took off and ran for the deepest woods, their tails between their legs and their ears flattened. The leader paused for one moment, watching the pack go. He glanced back toward the bushes where Jack stood hidden. Then he, too, turned tail and ran.

There was one more thing Jack had to do. He searched his memory for the sound of a voice he'd heard on Maisie's street. "Tracker!" he called, in that boy's voice. "Tracker, come on home, girl!"

In a moment, the spotted dog reappeared at the edge of the clearing. Her eyes met Jack's. They were full of hope.

"You don't belong here," he told her. "Let's go home."

Jack was exhausted, but he was alive. Now it was time to find his way back to Maisie.

With Tracker following close behind, Jack set off at a steady trot, back the way he'd run the day before. It seemed to take forever to find the path through tangled underbrush, over rushing streams, and between the tall trees of the oldest part of the forest. But finally, the two dogs came to the edge of Tinsdale.

Tracker paused and gave Jack a grateful look. Then she dashed off, heading eagerly for home.

Jack was too tired to run. Slowly, he limped down the street. His tongue hung out as he panted from exhaustion and thirst. His coat was tangled and filthy. With a last burst of energy, he walked up to Maisie's porch. He lifted one sore paw and scratched at the door.

Seconds later, the door flew open. "Jack!" cried Maisie. "Oh, Jack!"

"Mai—arf!" Jack said, catching himself just in time. A whole crowd of children appeared behind Maisie and looked down at him. The Ackermans! From next door. That was new.

Maisie dropped to her knees and threw her arms around Jack's bony body. "You're back," she whispered into the matted fur of his neck. "You're back."

"And he looks as if he's been through plenty," said Andrew.

Maisie's parents came out onto the porch to see what was happening. When she saw Jack, Mother gasped — then put on a fake smile. Father just harrumphed. They both pretended not to see the Ackermans.

Maisie brought Jack inside and fed him until he couldn't eat any more. Then Alison helped her brush the worst of the snarls out of his coat.

Aaron and Adam promised to help give him a bath the next day, and Annie gave him a brand-new tennis ball she'd been saving just for him. He curled up on his bed and slept and slept and slept.

When he woke up, Jack and Maisie were alone and free to talk. Jack told Maisie a little about what had happened to him, and Maisie told Jack that, now that he was back, she was the happiest girl in the world.

"I have friends now," she said, as if she still couldn't quite believe it. She told him all about how wonderful the Ackermans had been when he was gone.

"What about your parents?" Jack asked.

"What about them?" Maisie said defiantly. "They'll have to get used to me having friends."

Jack was relieved. If Maisie had the Ackermans for company, she wouldn't need him to talk anymore. He could keep his resolution and go back to being a regular dog. He could sleep and eat and chase squirrels and bark like any other dog, instead of talking. Which is exactly what he did.

Except for every once in a while, on a snowy day

or a rainy afternoon, when he would tell Maisie stories.

And every once in a while, Maisie and her friends would crowd into the Ackermans' cozy little playhouse, bringing in lemonade and sandwiches, and dog biscuits for Jack. First, they would play cards for a while, loud, rollicking games of rummy or go fish. Afterward, everybody would settle into the musty old chairs and couches, and Maisie would tell them the stories that Jack had told her: the tall tales, the fairy tales, the yarns about adventure on the high seas, and the stories of wild animals and their ways.

■ ■ ■

At that exact moment, the bell rang. School was over and it was time to go home. Mr. Taylor smiled. "That's it," he said, holding up his hands. "The end."

"But —" Oliver began.

"We'll talk about it Monday," Mr. Taylor promised, getting up to turn off the light. "Right now you all need to get your things together and head for home."

The End

Cricket could hardly wait until sharing time on Monday morning. It turned out that she wasn't the only one.

A minute after the morning bell rang, Leo burst into the classroom. He was wearing a huge smile. "Guess what!" he shouted. "Tracker's back!"

Everybody cheered.

"That's excellent news, Leo," said Mr. Taylor as everybody sat down in a circle on the floor for sharing time. "Tell us more about it." Cricket noticed that Mr. Taylor had a notebook on his lap: the big red *Taylor-Made Tales* notebook she'd seen on his desk on the first day he appeared in their classroom. She could hardly believe that was only a week ago. She felt as if she'd known Mr. Taylor forever.

"It happened Friday night," Leo said, "after

dinner. I was helping my dad clean up the kitchen when we both heard this scratching at the door." Leo paused. "I was almost too scared to go look," he said, in a low voice. "I mean, I don't think I could have stood it if it wasn't Tracker. But it was! She came back, just like the Tracker in the story." Leo beamed.

Cricket was happy to see her friend acting like his old self again. It seemed that everyone had found their lost things. And Molly was even going to get to see Ms. Nelson later that day: Mr. Taylor had put a note on the blackboard saying she was coming to pay a visit with her brand-new baby boy.

"That was so cool, how all our lost things were in your story," Jason said to Mr. Taylor.

"Just one of my many talents," said Mr. Taylor, stretching his long arms overhead. He smiled. "You should see me play basketball."

Molly raised her hand. "Was . . . was it magic that everybody's things got found?"

Mr. Taylor laughed. "It wasn't magic. It was

just luck," he answered. "Really good luck." He smiled at Leo.

"Could you tell other stories?" Jennifer asked. "Like, if we gave you a list of things to put in them?"

"Absolutely." Mr. Taylor looked pleased to be asked. "In fact, I want each of you to be working on a list of, let's say, five items, for future stories. We'll take turns until everybody's had a chance to hear his or her very own Taylor-Made Tale. After we hear the stories, they'll be in this book so we can read them again and again." He held up the red notebook and opened it to a page near the end. "The Dog's Secret," it said on the page, and underneath the title was a picture of a black dog sitting next to a brown-haired little girl.

Cricket could hardly wait to hear the next story. *Taylor-Made Tales*. That was perfect. Like tailor-made, when somebody sews a suit that is custom-made to your personal measurements. Only Mr. Taylor sewed stories, custom-made ones. Out of any five things you could think of!

Everybody started to shout out ideas for things they wanted Mr. Taylor to put into a story.

"A pirate ship!" yelled Leo. "Hey, do you know how much it cost the pirate to have his ears pierced? A buck an ear! Get it? A buccaneer? Like a pirate?"

Cricket groaned. But she smiled at her friend. It was good to hear Leo cracking jokes again.

"A bag full of money," said Jason, rubbing his hands together. "Like, thousands and thousands of dollars."

"And a wishing well!" Molly added, without even raising her hand. "So you could wish for even more good stuff!"

Mr. Taylor just smiled and nodded. "Great ideas!" he said. "But hold on to them. Write them down. Keep a list. We'll have time for lots of stories."

Jennifer raised her hand. "Was that story true?" she asked. "I mean, a dog can't really talk, can it? I think Maisie was just pretending Jack could talk. She made up all that stuff about his adventures to explain why he was gone so long."

"Well," said Mr. Taylor, "that's the great thing about stories: Anything can happen. Anyway, all I can tell you is that everybody in my family is a good storyteller, but my grandma knew more stories than anybody I ever met. Her name was Annie. Annie Ackerman, until she met and married my grandpa Taylor."

Cricket's mouth fell open. "Little Annie was your grandma?" she asked, without even *thinking* about raising her hand, or waiting her turn, or blending in instead of sticking out. She jumped to her feet. "I want to hear *all* her stories. Tell another one!"

Mr. Taylor didn't frown at her. He didn't tell her to raise her hand. He just laughed. "All in good time, Kathryn," he promised.

All of a sudden, Cricket realized something. Mr. Taylor wasn't like other teachers. He didn't care very much about all the usual things, like Being Mature and Raising Your Hand and Waiting Your Turn. Mr. Taylor would like Cricket just as much as Kathryn — in fact, he would probably like Cricket even *better*. She could give up trying to follow all those stupid Steps, and just be herself.

And that made Cricket very, very happy.

"You can call me Cricket," she said with a big smile.

Mr. Taylor smiled back. "Cricket it is," he said. "I think that name suits you perfectly." Then he stood up and stretched out his long, long arms. He reached over to turn out the lamp. "And now," he said, "I think it's time for some math."

About the Author

Ellen Miles has always loved a good story. She also loves biking, skiing, writing, and playing with her dog, Django. Django is a black Lab who would rather eat a book than read one.

Don't miss the next thrilling adventure!

TAYLOR-MADE TALES

by
ELLEN MILES

Give new teacher Mr. Taylor a pirate ship, a brass key, a six-toed cat, a hunk of cheese, and a mop, and he spins a seafaring tale of a young stowaway who's up to his neck in trouble. Can the boy survive a mutiny and help the captain save the ship from pirates?